Better Move On, Frog!

Ron Maris

Discovery Toys, Inc.

This edition is
published and distributed
exclusively by
Discovery Toys, Inc.
Martinez, CA

First published in Great Britain
in 1982 by Julia MacRae Books
A division of Walker Books Ltd., London

© Ron Maris 1982

Printed in Italy

ISBN 0-939979-33-0

For Pat Hutchins

Holes! Lots of holes!
Which one shall I use?

Better move on, Frog.
This hole is full of badgers.

Better move on, Frog.
This hole is full of rabbits.

Better move on, Frog.
This hole is full of owls.

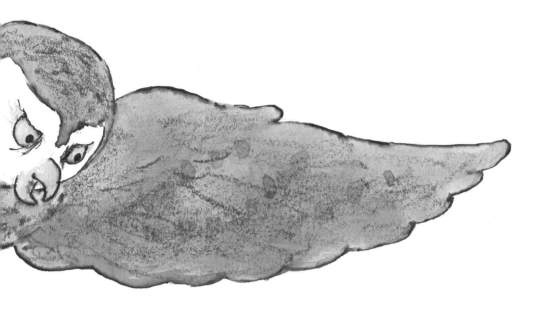

Better move on, Frog.
This hole is full of mice.

Better move on, Frog.
This hole is full of bees.

But look!

Better move in, Frog.
And wait for the hole to fill up...

...like all the other holes.

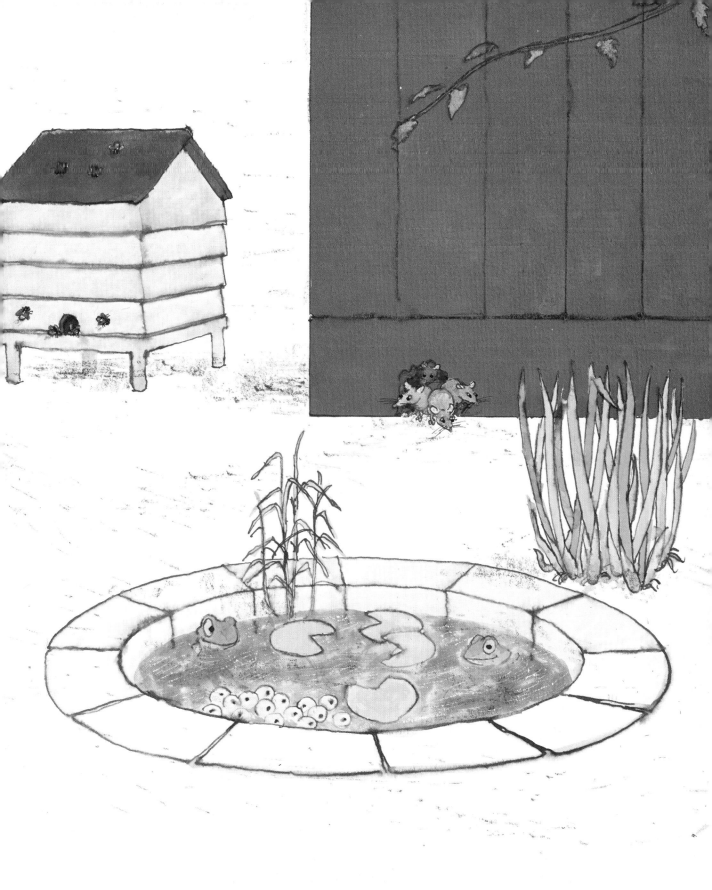